Things Bunny Sees

By Cyndy Szekeres

A Golden Book • New York
Western Publishing Company, Inc., Racine, Wisconsin 53404

Bunny is with Daddy.

Bunny sees something green.

Bunny sees Daddy working.

Bunny sees something yellow.

Bunny wants to have fun!

Bunny sees something blue.

Daddy helps Bunny.

Bunny sees little black things.

Mother calls Bunny to come in.

Bunny sees some red things.

He makes a big house.

He sees something hot.

Bunny and Mother look at a book.

Bunny sees something brown.

Bunny sees something big.

What does Bunny see now?
He sees a good little bunny!